Where's That cat?

Margaret K. McElderry Books
An imprint of Simon & Schuster Children's Publishing Division
1230 Avenue of the Americas
New York, NY 10020

Book design by Michael Nelson.
The text of this book is set in Adobe Nueva MM.
The illustrations are rendered in watercolor.

Printed in Hong Kong
2 4 6 8 10 9 7 5 3 1

Library of Congress Cataloging-in-Publication Data
Merriam, Eve, 1916-1992.
Where's That Cat? / by Eve Merriam and Pam Pollack; illustrated by Joanna Harrison.—1st ed.
p. cm.
Summary: A girl chases her cat, Jitterbugs, out of the house, around the park, and back home again.
ISBN 0-689-82904-3
[1. Cats—Fiction. 2. Parks—Fiction. 3. Stories in rhyme.] I. Pollack, Pamela. II. Harrison, Joanna, ill. III. Title.
PZ8.3.M55187 Ji 2000 [E]—dc21 99-46925

FIRST
EDITION

Eve Merriam and Pam Pollack

Where's That Cat?

illustrated by

Joanna Harrison

Margaret K. McElderry Books
New York London Toronto Sydney Singapore

Jitterbugs, Jitterbugs jumps to the floor.
Under the table — *tap tap tap!*

Out of sight,

now where's that cat?

Under the table, on my knees—

what *Squeaks* open and makes a breeze?

Jitterbugs, Jitterbugs *glides* out the door,

onto the road—he's far away,
looking for a place to play.

Down the road,

I walk really *fast*.

What's white and runs along the grass?

Jitterbugs, Jitterbugs *climbs* up the fence,

over a puddle—*me-ow-ow!*

Where could he
be hiding now?

Over the puddle, following.

What's **ticklish**, green, and smells like spring?

Jitterbugs, Jitterbugs **rolls** in the grass.

Up into the air—just like that!

Gone with a **whoosh**—where's that cat?

Onto my head, leaves *flutter* down.
What's tall as the sky and touches the ground?

Jitterbugs, Jitterbugs *leaps* from the tree,

over a stream to the other side,
looking for a place to hide.

Now I *jump* over to explore.
What stands with feet on either shore?

Jitterbugs, Jitterbugs crosses the bridge.
Up the hill, way up high.

Gone again—*OH, NO! OH, MY!*

I stand up on my *ti**pp**y-toes*.

What's strong and still
when the wind blows?

Jitterbugs, Jitterbugs *jumps* off the rock,

down the hill, *fast* as can be!

Who's that coming after me?

Besides the grass so soft and sweet, what's hard and dry beneath our feet?

Jitterbugs, Jitterbugs **r u n s** down the road,

into the yard. I'm right behind.

Back again, what will he find?

Through the window, look and see—

where's the very best place you can be?

Jitterbugs, Jitterbugs comes back home,

into my arms with hugs to share,

purring, **_purring_** everywhere.

Where's a good place to take a nap?

Jitterbugs, Jitterbugs in my lap.